Disney
THE LION KING

I JUST CAN'T WAIT TO BE KING

Illustrated by Steph Laberis
Designed by Maureen Mulligan

"I Just Can't Wait to Be King"
Music by Elton John, Lyrics by Tim Rice
Published by Wonderland Music Company, Inc. (BMI). All rights reserved.

SUSTAINABLE
FORESTRY
INITIATIVE
Certified Sourcing
www.sfiprogram.org
SFI-00993
Logo Applies to Text Stock Only

Disney PRESS
LOS ANGELES • NEW YORK

I'M gonna be a
MIGHTY KING,
SO enemies
BEWARE.

Well, I've NEVER seen a KING of BEASTS with QUITE so LITTLE ▲▲▲▲▲ HAIR.

I'M gonna be the MANE event, ♪ like NO KING was BEFORE. I'M brushing UP on looking down. I'M WORKING on MY ROAR!

Thus far, a rather UNINSPIRING thing. OH, I just can't wait to be KING! ♪♪ You've rather a LONG WAY to go, young MASTER, if you THINK—

No one saying,
"DO THIS." ♫
NOW when I
SAID that, I—
No one saying,
"BE THERE."
What I MEANT was—

No one saying,
"STOP THAT."
LOOK, WHAT YOU
don't realize—
No one saying,
"SEE HERE."
Now SEE HERE!

FREE to RUN
around all DAY!
Well, that's definitely out.
FREE to DO IT
ALL MY WAY!

I THINK it's TIME that YOU and I ARRANGED A heart to heart.

KINGS don't **NEED** **ADVICE** from little **HORNBILLS** for a start. ♫

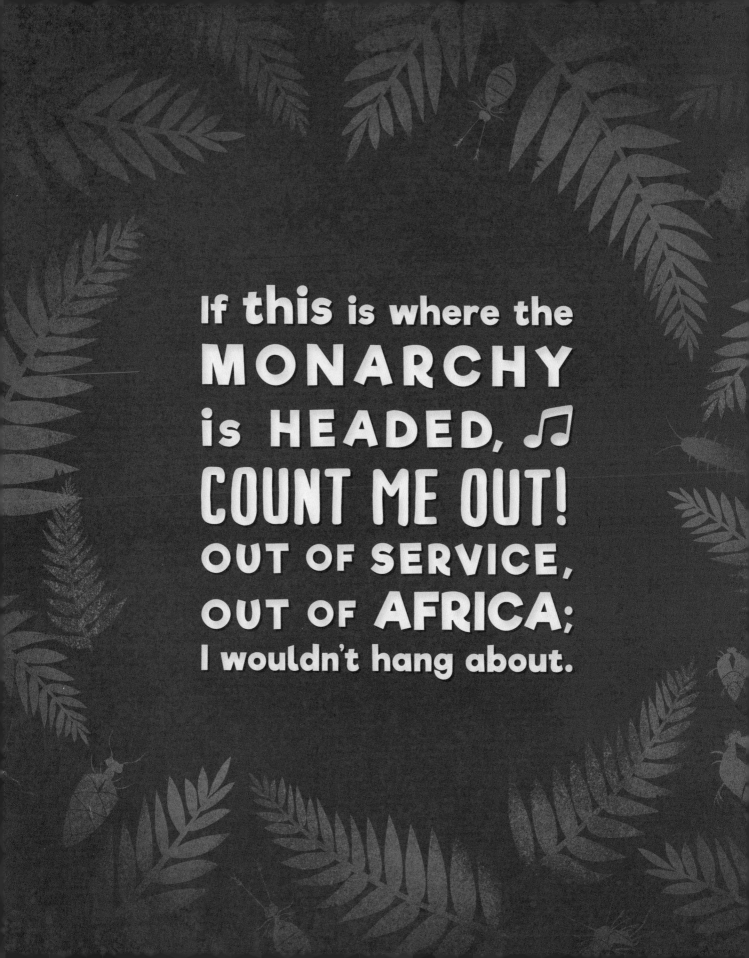

If **this** is where the **MONARCHY** is **HEADED**, ♫ **COUNT ME OUT!** **OUT OF SERVICE, OUT OF AFRICA;** I wouldn't hang about.

This CHILD is getting WILDLY OUT of WING. OH, I just can't wait to be KING!

EVERYBODY ← look left. **EVERYBODY** look right. → **EVERYWHERE** you LOOK I'M STANDIN' in the SPOTLIGHT. NOT YET!

♫ Let EVERY CREATURE go for broke and sing. Let's HEAR IT in the HERD and ON THE ||: WING. :||

OH, I just CAN'T WAIT to be ♫♪ KING!

OH, I just CAN'T WAIT to be ♫ KING!